# Stone Underpants

By **Rebecca Lisle**

Illustrated by **Richard Watson**

It was cold in the Stone Age.

When the icy wind blew, it was freezing.

"I really do need something to keep my bottom warm," Pod told his Dad.

"You could make something," Dad said. "Why not make it out of stone?"

So Pod got to work on a big block of stone.

Pod made himself some super stone underpants.

"Yahoo! These are great!" he cried.

He put them on and went out to play.

But Pod couldn't run wearing the stone

underpants. He couldn't kick or bend.

He came down with a THUMP!

His friends were cross.

"Oh Pod! Now the others have scored a goal!"

Pod and his friends went to the lake. They all jumped in. His friends bobbed back up...

But Pod sank down.

Pod threw his stone underpants away.

"So much for the Stone Age!" he said.

Pod had another go. This time he used **wood**.

Pod cut and he sawed.

He hammered and he nailed.

And he made himself a pair

of **wooden** underpants.

They were light and airy. But they were very

scratchy and splintery!

Pod's wooden underpants didn't last long.

In the night they mysteriously disappeared.

"Stone's no good. Wood's no use. But I still need some bottom warmers!" Pod said. What could he try next?

Shells were too **spiky**.

Spider webs were too **sticky**.

Mud was too **yucky** - and it was full of worms!

Birds flew down to eat the worms.

"Hey! Watch out with those beaks!"

Pod cried. "Don't eat me!"

But the birds gave Pod an idea. "Feathers!"

Pod gathered up as many feathers as he

could... Not every bird wanted to share.

At last Pod had enough.

So he got to work on the big heap of feathers.

The fluffy feather underpants were light and soft and deliciously **warm**. When he went out to play football he could run... jump... and kick.

But...

The feather underpants were so itchy; he
twitched and twisted. He squirmed and
wriggled. The feather underpants
were too **ticklish** for Pod...

But his mum really liked them.

Pod wondered if he'd ever get any underpants.

What a lovely
feather duster.

"Hello, warm, woolly mammoth," said Pod,

patting the friendly mammoth.

"Oh, your lovely coat's given me a great idea!"

Pod's needles clicked and clacked.

He knitted and knotted and he made himself...

# Woolly underpants!

Now climbing trees was a doddle.

Kicking balls was brilliant.

Swimming was super. And best of all...

"My bottom is so TOASTY!" cried Pod.

"Goodbye Stone Age!

I love the Wool Age!"

# Quiz

1. It was _____ in the Stone Age?
a) Boring
b) Cold
c) Exciting

2. What happens when Pod wears his stone underpants?
a) He cannot kick or bend
b) He scores a goal
c) He breaks them

3.  Why do shells not make good underpants?
a) They are too shiny
b) They are too wet
c) They are too spiky

4. What does Pod's mum use his feather underpants as?

a) A feather duster

b) A hat

c) A scarf

5. Where does Pod get the wool?

a) A sheep

b) A woolly mammoth

c) A bird

*Turn over for answers*

# Book Bands for Guided Reading

The Institute of Education book banding system is a scale of colours that reflects the various levels of reading difficulty. The bands are assigned by taking into account the content, the language style, the layout and phonics.

Maverick Early Readers are a bright, attractive range of books covering the pink to purple bands. All of these books have been book banded for guided reading to the industry standard and edited by a leading educational consultant.

For more titles visit:
www.maverickbooks.co.uk/early-readers

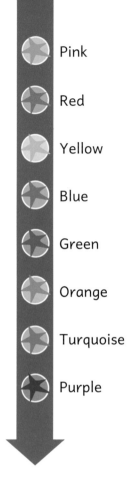

Pink

Red

Yellow

Blue

Green

Orange

Turquoise

Purple

Book Band — Purple

| A Right Royal Mess | 978-1-84886-298-2 |
| Stone Underpants | 978-1-84886-297-5 |
| Biscuit Blast Off! | 978-1-84886-236-4 |
| The Great Grizzly Race | 978-1-84886-239-5 |
| The Jelly That Wouldn't Wobble | 978-1-84886-225-8 |

*Quiz Answers: 1b, 2a, 3c, 4a, 5b*